NBA CHAMPIONSHIP:

↓

1977

↓

ALL-TIME LEADING SCORER:

↓

CLYDE DREXLER (1983–95):

↓

18,040 POINTS

THE NBA: A HISTORY OF HOOPS

PORTLAND TRAIL BLAZERS

NETS
43

THE NBA: A HISTORY OF HOOPS

PORTLAND TRAIL BLAZERS

BY JIM WHITING

CREATIVE EDUCATION CREATIVE PAPERBACKS

Published by Creative Education
and Creative Paperbacks

P.O. Box 227, Mankato, Minnesota 56002

Creative Education and Creative Paperbacks
are imprints of The Creative Company

www.thecreativecompany.us

Design by Blue Design; production by Joe Kahnke

Printed in the United States of America

Photographs by Alamy (ZUMA Press, Inc.), AP Images (ASSOCIATED PRESS), Getty Images (Andrew D. Bernstein/NBAE, Bettmann, Jonathan Ferrey/Getty Images Sport, Focus on Sport/Getty Images Sport, Sam Forencich/NBAE, JOHN GRESS/AFP, Andy Hayt/Sports Illustrated, Thearon W. Henderson/Getty Images Sport, Walter Iooss Jr./Sports Illustrated, Layne Murdoch/NBAE, Ezra Shaw/Getty Images Sport, UCLA/Collegiate Images), iStockphoto (chinaface)

Library of Congress Cataloging-in-Publication Data

Names: Whiting, Jim, 1943- author.

Title: Portland Trail Blazers / Jim Whiting.

Series: The NBA: A History of Hoops.

Includes bibliographical references and index.

Summary: This high-interest title summarizes the history of the Portland Trail Blazers professional basketball team, highlighting memorable events and noteworthy players such as Bill Walton.

Identifiers: LCCN 2017009412 / ISBN 978-1-60818-859-8 (hardcover) / ISBN 978-1-62832-462-4 (pbk) / ISBN 978-1-56660-907-4 (eBook)

Subjects: LCSH: 1. Portland Trail Blazers (Basketball team)—History—Juvenile literature. 2. Portland Trail Blazers (Basketball team)—Biography—Juvenile literature.

Classification: LCC GV885.52.P67 W45 2017 / DDC 796.323/640979549—dc23

CCSS: RI.4.1, 2, 3, 4; RI.5.1, 2, 4; RI.6.1, 2, 3; RF.4.3, 4; RF.5.3, 4; RH. 6-8. 4, 5, 7

First Edition HC 9 8 7 6 5 4 3 2 1

First Edition PBK 9 8 7 6 5 4 3 2 1

RIP CITY UPRISE
PLAYOFFS 2009
JUST DO IT, PORTLAND!
Rebecca Watts
THEY SAID WE WERE TOO YOUNG
WE SHOWED THEM

RISE WITH US
HUSTLEBOARD
BLOCKED SHOTS
REBOUNDS
STEALS
TOTAL
BLAZERS FANS
STATS CENTRAL
FIELD GOAL PCT.
FREE THROW PCT.
FREE THROWS MADE
3 - POINT PCT.
3 - POINTERS MADE
OFF REBOUNDS
2ND CHANCE PTS.
PACIFIC OFFICE AUTOMATION
Pizza Hut
OICE & HIGH SPEED INTERN
BUSINESS
BLAZERS
10
ROCKETS
PLAYOFFS

CONTENTS

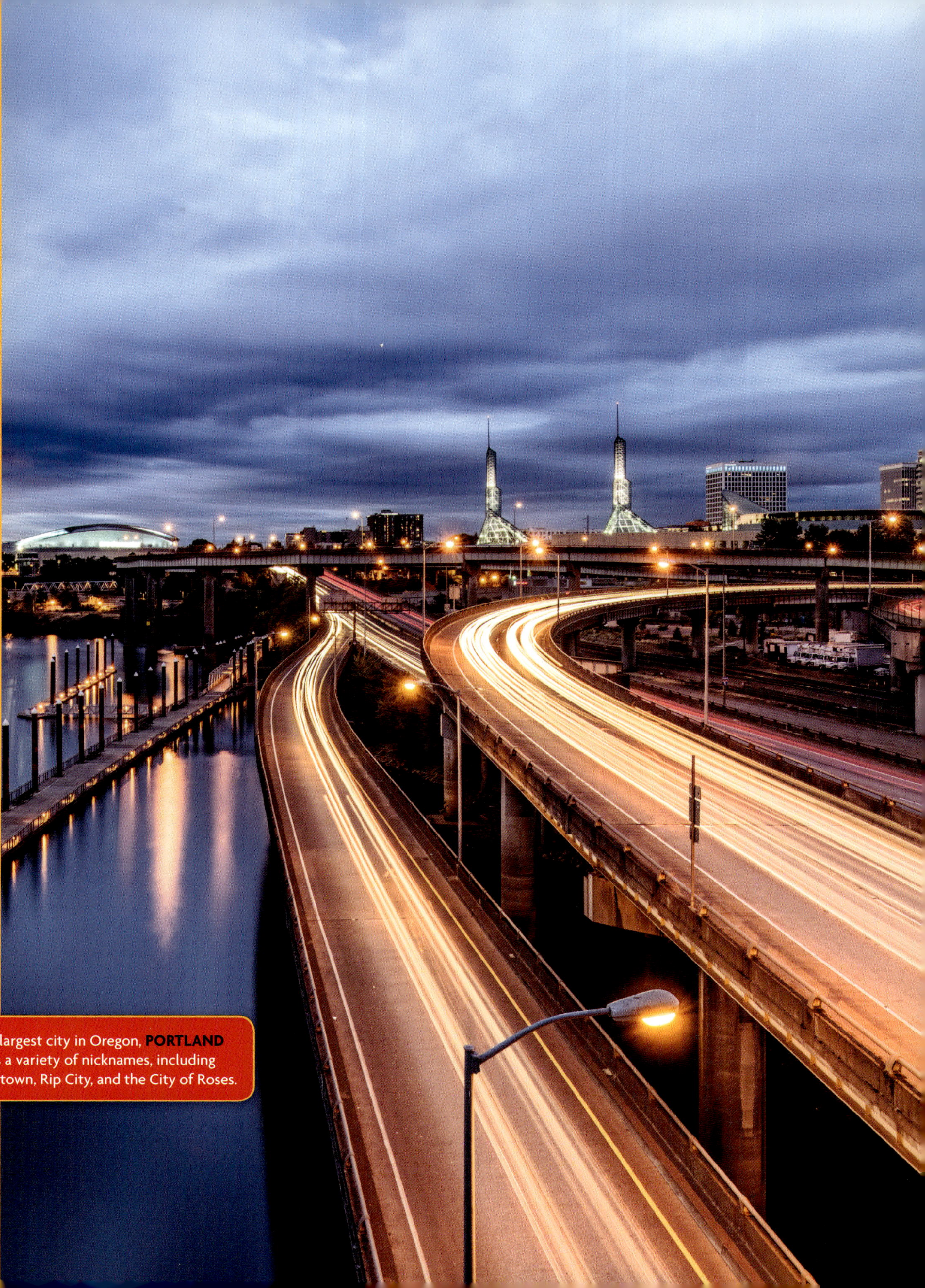

The largest city in Oregon, **PORTLAND** has a variety of nicknames, including Stumptown, Rip City, and the City of Roses.

BLAZING A TRAIL TO THE TOP

By 4:30 A.M. on June 5, 1977, more than 5,000 fans were waiting at the Portland, Oregon, airport. They wanted to greet the Portland Trail Blazers. The team had defeated the Philadelphia 76ers the previous night in Game 5 of the National Basketball Association (NBA) Finals. Philadelphia had dominated the first two games of the series. But Portland crushed the Sixers in the next two. The Game 5 win put Portland in the driver's seat. "When we got off that plane and we saw the level of support and the level of commitment, there was no way we were ever going to give up," said Blazers center Bill Walton.

Home fans roared their approval the next night at Game 6. The Blazers jumped out to a 12-point halftime lead. Philadelphia didn't quit, though. They closed to within two points with eight seconds remaining. A Sixer fired up a shot that would tie the score. No good. Another shot. No good. A third shot. Still no good. Walton controlled the rebound as time ran out. The Blazers were world champs! Walton had 20 points, 23 rebounds, 8 blocked shots, and 7 assists. He

Tireless center **BILL WALTON** led the Blazers to the NBA title in 1977.

Portland's first draft pick, **GEOFF PETRIE**, had the potential for greatness but retired early from injuries.

was named the Most Valuable Player (MVP) of the Finals. Walton ripped off his jersey and hurled it into the stands. "If I had caught the shirt, I would have eaten it," said teammate Maurice Lucas. "Bill's my hero."

Along with Cleveland and Buffalo, the city of Portland was granted an NBA expansion franchise in 1970. A name-the-team contest attracted more than 10,000 entries. "Pioneers" was the most popular choice. But nearby Lewis & Clark College already used that name. So team officials went with another popular entry: Trail Blazers. The name referred to the Lewis and Clark expedition. It had passed through the region in 1805 on the way to the Pacific Ocean. Club executive Harry Glickman said the name "reflects both the ruggedness of the Pacific Northwest and the start of a major league era in our state." Not everyone shared Glickman's excitement. "It really wasn't very popular when fans first heard it, but of course we all know that changed," he added. Many people shortened the name to Blazers. Terms such as "Go Blazers" and "Blazermania" quickly caught on in Portland.

Like all NBA expansion teams, the Blazers struggled in their first years. They won just 29 games in 1970–71. The following season they slipped to 18 victories. They did have back-to-back Rookies of the Year. Sharpshooting guard Geoff Petrie earned the award in 1971, and versatile forward Sidney Wicks did the same in 1972. But there wasn't enough

With the size of a center and speed of a forward, **SIDNEY WICKS** was called "Mr. Everything."

talent surrounding the two players. The Blazers continued to finish at the bottom of the Western Conference. They also wasted most of their high draft picks on bad choices.

LEGENDS OF THE HARDWOOD

"RIP CITY"

During Portland's first season, the team was playing the Los Angeles Lakers. Blazers guard Jim Barnett drained a long jump shot. Radio play-by-play announcer Bill Schonely shouted "Rip City—all right!" into the microphone. Scorekeeper Jeff Wohler asked him where the phrase came from. Schonely replied, "I don't know—it just came out." Wohler said, "Well, leave it in." The phrase quickly became a symbol of the franchise and the city. "Rip City" T-shirts and other apparel are best-sellers in the official team store. Schonely retired in 1998. Yet today he is still referred to as "the mayor of Rip City."

UCLA
32

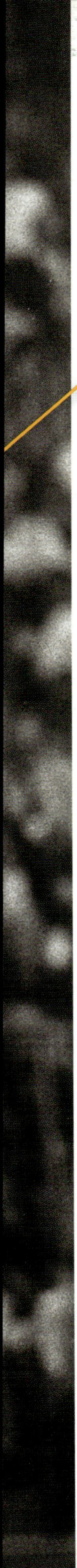

WALTON's struggle with injuries began in high school and followed him throughout his career.

BILL WALTON TO THE RESCUE

The 1974 NBA Draft was a different story. The 76ers had finished last in the Eastern Conference. The Blazers sat at the bottom of the Western Conference for the fourth year in a row. The

The 1977–78 Blazers finished atop the NBA but could not find their way to the Finals.

teams flipped a coin to see who would choose first in the Draft. The Blazers won. They selected UCLA center Bill Walton. He was a three-time College Player of the Year. He led the Bruins to two national championships. Portland fans expected immediate success when he joined the team. They didn't get it. Walton struggled with injuries. At various times, he broke his nose, foot, and wrist. "For two years, I wasn't able to run up and down the court freely without … thinking about [my injuries]," Walton explained. "That's no way to play basketball." He played just 35 games as a rookie and 51 the following season. The Blazers won 38 games his first year and 37 the second. But the team did escape from the Western Conference basement.

In 1976, Portland hired no-nonsense coach Jack Ramsay. He emphasized defense and a team-first attitude. He also benefited from

blazers
25
blazers
20
blazers
32
blazers
10
blazers
30
blazers
24
13
23

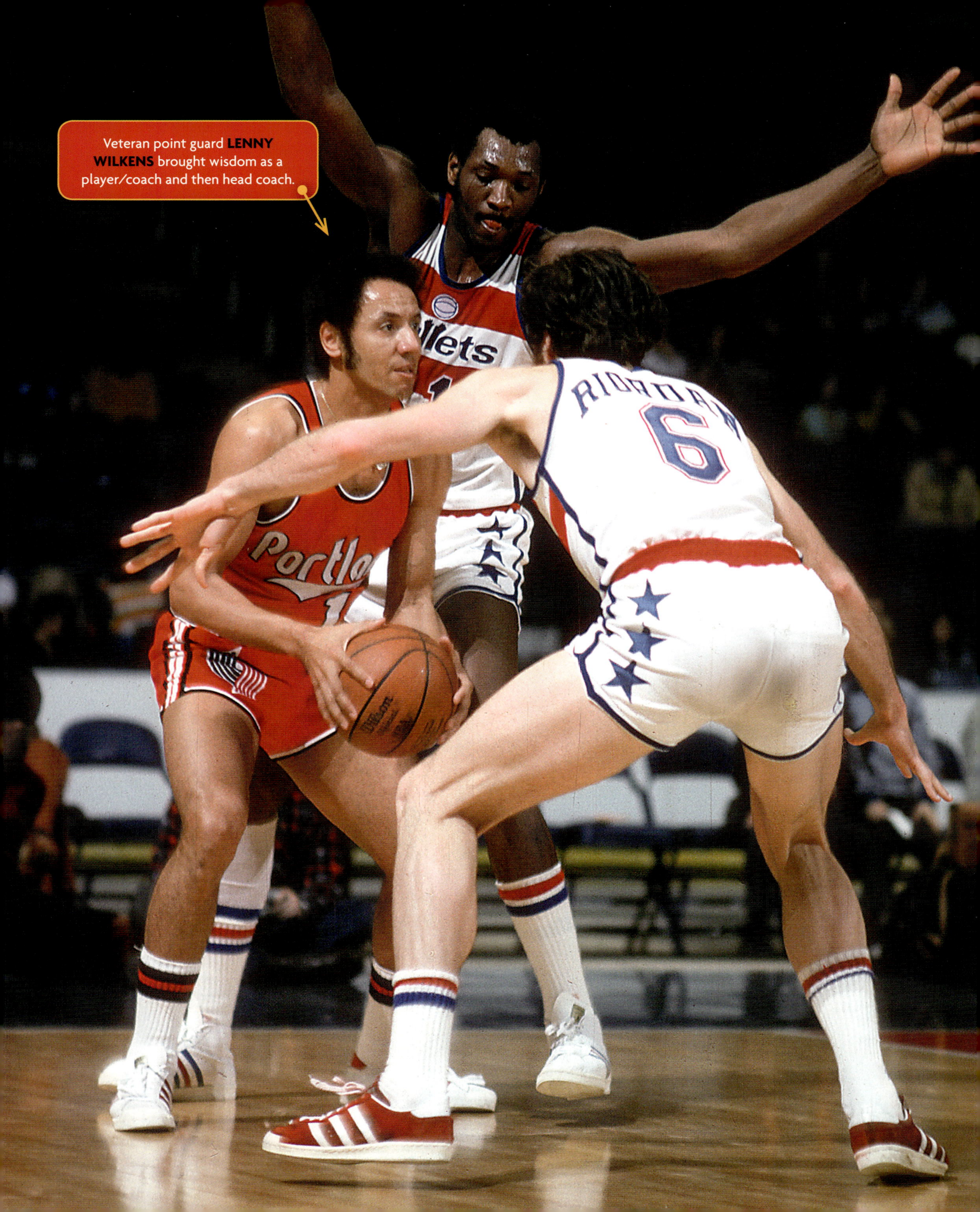

Veteran point guard **LENNY WILKENS** brought wisdom as a player/coach and then head coach.

> "THE FANS ... PROVIDED A CONSTANT DIN OF SUPPORT. FOR A COACH, THERE COULDN'T HAVE BEEN A BETTER ENVIRONMENT."

the support of the "Blazermaniacs." The faithful fans believed in the team, even though they had yet to enjoy a winning season. "The whole atmosphere in Portland was a huge psychological lift for me and the players," said Ramsay. "The fans ... provided a constant din of support. For a coach, there couldn't have been a better environment." Walton was finally healthy. Portland won 49 games. It was the team's first winning season. The Blazers cruised through the playoffs. They defeated the Chicago Bulls and the Denver Nuggets in the first two rounds. Then they swept the Los Angeles Lakers in the Western Conference finals. They completed the season by winning the NBA championship. It was the first time a team had won the title in its first playoff appearance.

The Blazers did even better in the 1977–78 season. They won 58 games. That was the best record in the NBA. Walton was named

Nicknamed "Big Red" for his fiery hair and personality, **WALTON** could shoot, block, and pass with ease.

the league's MVP. Fans were confident of back-to-back titles. But the injury bug bit Walton again. He broke his foot early in the playoffs. Without him, the Blazers bowed out. After that, Walton claimed the team's medical staff hadn't given him proper treatment. He demanded a trade. He didn't get it. So he sat out the entire 1978–79 season. The team traded him to the San Diego Clippers. He was hurt even more there. "If Bill Walton is healthy, he undoubtedly would go down as one of the five best centers of all-time," Petrie said. "There was nobody like him."

LEGENDS OF THE HARDWOOD

OFF-COURT INTERESTS

BILL WALTON, CENTER, 6-FOOT-11, 1974–78

Bill Walton made headlines for more than his basketball skills. He was arrested in his junior year at UCLA during a Vietnam War protest. His coach bailed him out of jail. A vegetarian who wore flannel shirts, he carried his gear in a burlap bag. Walton loved rock music, too. He especially enjoyed the Grateful Dead. He attended more than 850 of the band's concerts. He was nicknamed the "Big Red Deadhead" for his height, hair color, and band choice. Growing up, Walton stuttered and was shy. He overcame those issues. Today he announces basketball telecasts. Everyone else wears a suit. Walton wears tie-dyed T-shirts.

Guard **JIM PAXSON** led Portland in scoring for two seasons in the 1980s.

WELCOME TO THE GLIDE

The Blazers made center Mychal Thompson the first overall pick in the 1978 NBA Draft. He made the All-Rookie first team. Together with guard Jim Paxson, the team's top draft choice in 1979, he helped

CLYDE "THE GLIDE" DREXLER soared to the basket with exciting slam dunks and lay-ins.

the Blazers to the playoffs the next three seasons. They were stopped in the first round each time. After missing the playoffs in 1981–82, the Blazers surged back. They advanced to the conference semifinals before losing. Portland struck an especially rich lode of gold in the 1983 NBA Draft. It picked up shooting guard Clyde Drexler. "The Glide," as he was soon called, was not very smooth during his first season. He averaged fewer than eight points a game. The road became much smoother the

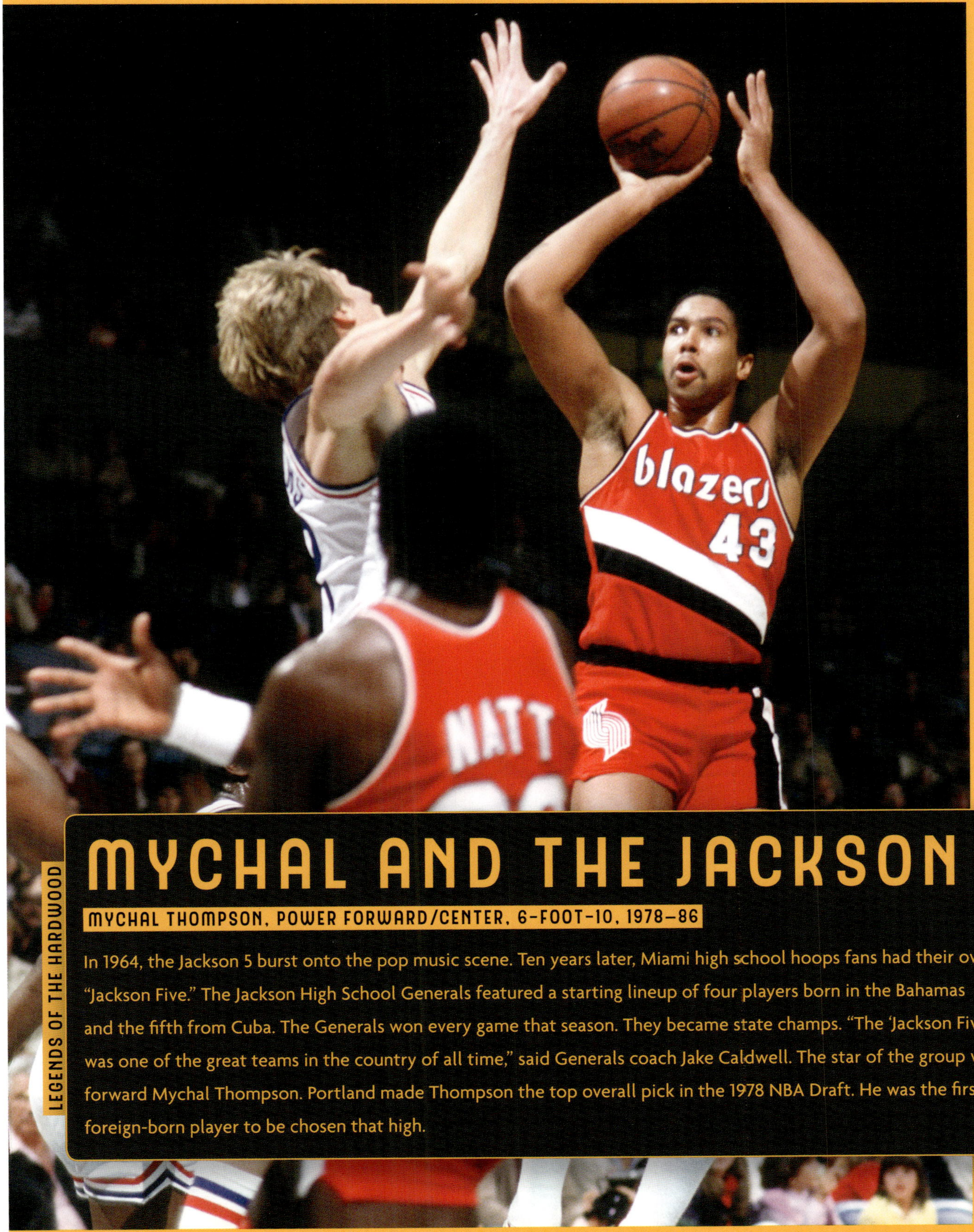

LEGENDS OF THE HARDWOOD

MYCHAL AND THE JACKSON 5

MYCHAL THOMPSON, POWER FORWARD/CENTER, 6-FOOT-10, 1978–86

In 1964, the Jackson 5 burst onto the pop music scene. Ten years later, Miami high school hoops fans had their own "Jackson Five." The Jackson High School Generals featured a starting lineup of four players born in the Bahamas and the fifth from Cuba. The Generals won every game that season. They became state champs. "The 'Jackson Five' was one of the great teams in the country of all time," said Generals coach Jake Caldwell. The star of the group was forward Mychal Thompson. Portland made Thompson the top overall pick in the 1978 NBA Draft. He was the first foreign-born player to be chosen that high.

LEGENDS OF THE HARDWOOD

A HIGHFLYING FRATERNITY

CLYDE DREXLER, SHOOTING GUARD, 6-FOOT-7, 1983–95

The players at the University of Houston in the early 1980s raced up and down the court. They were especially famous for their explosive slam dunks. A local sportswriter called them Phi Slama Jama. The name made them sound like they were a fraternity. Another nickname was "Texas's Tallest Fraternity." One of the leaders was 6-foot-7 Clyde Drexler. Drexler continued his highflying scoring punch when he arrived in Portland. "He was just the best athlete to ever play in Portland," said Blazers forward Steve Jones. "He could make a way when there was no way to be made." Drexler is Portland's all-time leading scorer.

following season. Drexler began a steady rise toward becoming one of the league's top scorers. In the 1985 playoffs, the Blazers stomped the Dallas Mavericks in the first round. But they lost to the Lakers after that. Portland continued to make the playoffs the next four seasons. But each year it couldn't get past the first round.

In the 1989–90 season, Portland won a franchise-best 59 games. The Blazers faced the powerful Detroit Pistons in the NBA Finals. Detroit won four out of five games. All but one game was decided by six points or fewer. "We had six new people on this team this year, and we reached the NBA Finals," said Drexler. "I just think the future looks so bright."

He was right. The Blazers won 19 of their first 20 games the following season. They finished with 63 victories. But they lost to the Lakers in the conference finals. "We're a better team than we showed," Drexler said. "We'll be back." Once again he was right. Portland returned to the Finals in 1992. This time it faced the Chicago Bulls. The media billed the series as a matchup between Drexler and Bulls superstar Michael Jordan. Jordan was the NBA's MVP that season. Drexler was runner-up. With Chicago leading the series 3–2, Portland took a 15-point lead in Game 6. If the Blazers hung on, they would force a deciding Game 7. Anything could happen then. But Chicago surged back for a 97–93 win and the NBA title. "Chicago's defensive intensity picked up, and we didn't handle the ball well," said coach Rick Adelman. "Our guys just ran out of gas."

They also seemed to run out of gas in the next six seasons. The Blazers continued to put up winning records. But they continued to lose in the first round of the playoffs. Several key players were traded. The biggest loss came midway through the 1994–95 season. Drexler had been an eight-time All-Star with Portland. Yet the team paid seven players more than it paid him. He demanded a trade and got it. "Clyde Drexler was the identity of the Portland Trail Blazers, and there will be no substitute," said teammate Terry Porter. Porter himself was gone a few months later.

All-Star point guard **TERRY PORTER** remains the all-time assists leader in Portland.

SUCCESS AND STRUGGLES

Portland made another run at the NBA title in the 1998–99 season. By then it had added several new players. The key newcomer was 7-foot-3 center Arvydas Sabonis. "Arvydas and Bill Walton are the two

Thanks in part to his towering height, **ARVYDAS SABONIS** was a skilled rebounder and shooter.

Seasoned forward **SCOTTIE PIPPEN** propelled Portland to the playoffs four times.

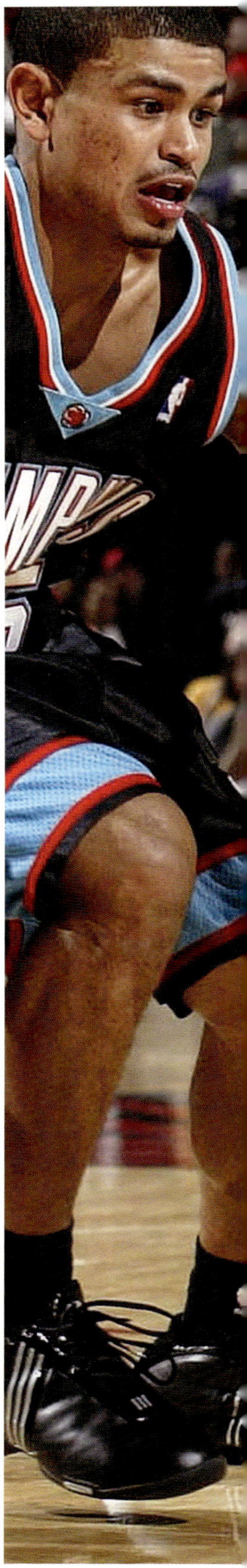

best passing big men ever," said coach Mike Dunleavy. "No one else is even close." With point guard Damon Stoudamire running the offense, the Blazers soared to the conference finals. Unfortunately, the San Antonio Spurs swept the series.

Portland traded for small forward Scottie Pippen soon afterward. Pippen had helped the Bulls win six NBA titles. His veteran leadership helped the Blazers return to the conference finals again. They lost three of the first four games to the Lakers. But Portland won the next two to tie the series. In Game 7, the Blazers built up a 15-point lead with just 10 minutes left in the game. Then they fell apart. "Portland choked jumper after jumper, shooting 22 percent for the period," writes Blazers historian Dave Deckard. "Nobody will forget the sickening feeling of watching that

Scrappy point guard **DAMON STOUDAMIRE** was a reliable floor leader.

The second overall pick in 2006, **LAMARCUS ALDRIDGE** fueled the Blazers with his scoring power.

10 minutes, of seeing the Blazers surrender the biggest Game 7 comeback in playoff history." The Lakers won 89–84.

That loss seemed to halt the team's progress. The Blazers made first-round exits in the next three seasons. Though the Blazers went 41–41 in 2003–04, they didn't qualify for the playoffs. That ended 21 straight postseason appearances. It was the second-longest streak in NBA history. (The Philadelphia 76ers had a streak of 22.) The playoffs remained out of reach for four more seasons. The Blazers hit bottom in 2005–06. They won just 21 games. It was their worst record since 1972–73. It was also the worst in the NBA that season.

Portland began laying the foundation for better things in 2006. It traded for power forward LaMarcus Aldridge and shooting guard Brandon Roy. Both players were named to the All-Rookie first team. Roy

HISTORY REPEATS ITSELF

LEGENDS OF THE HARDWOOD

Portland had the second overall choice in the 1984 Draft. It could have taken Michael Jordan. But the Blazers already had Clyde Drexler. They chose Sam Bowie instead. ESPN calls that the worst draft choice in *any* pro sport. “The Blazers should have known better: The 7-foot-1 center had missed two full seasons at Kentucky with a stress fracture in his left shinbone; sure enough, his NBA career was sabotaged by injuries,” wrote David Schoenfield. A similar situation arose in 2007. Portland could choose either injury-prone center Greg Oden (pictured) or lean sharpshooter Kevin Durant. Once again the Blazers took the big man. Oden played a total of 82 games in 5 years. Durant went on to a sensational career with the Oklahoma City Thunder and Golden State Warriors.

BRANDON ROY poured in nearly 20 points per game in Portland before injuries took their toll.

added Rookie of the Year to his honors. They helped the Blazers to 32 wins in their first season. In 2007–08, that number jumped to 41. The Blazers kept improving. They won 54 games in 2008–09. But once again, they couldn't get past the first round of the playoffs. This time they lost to the Houston Rockets, four games to two. The next two seasons were almost identical.

Roy had been bothered by knee problems since college. By the end of the 2010–11 season, it became apparent that the stress of long NBA seasons was too much. He announced his retirement. Without him, Portland won just 28 games.

Athletic point guard **DAMIAN LILLARD** showed steady improvement in Portland.

RIP CITY RESILIENCE

Once again the Blazers did well in the Draft. They took point guard Damian Lillard. He was named Rookie of the Year in 2013, though the Blazers missed the playoffs again. "[Lillard] keeps

BLAZERS
SPALDING
adidas

improving, and a lot of times it is in more subtle ways than looking at a box score," said coach Terry Stotts. "And he keeps doing what he's doing while becoming the focal point of the opponent's defense. That's not an easy thing to do." Lillard, Aldridge, and shooting guard Wesley Matthews sparked the Blazers to a 24–5 start in the 2013–14 season. But an injury to Aldridge poured cold water on that red-hot opening. They still finished with 54 wins and made it to the playoffs. Even without Aldridge, they managed to get past the first round. But San Antonio ended their season in the next round.

Halfway through the 2014–15 season, the Blazers were a scorching 30–11. But then Matthews tore his Achilles tendon. He was out for the season. "He's the heart and soul of this team," Aldridge said. Lillard added, "It's so much bigger than what he does on the floor. It's the energy he brings every day to the practice facility—the smile, cracking jokes." Portland still finished with 51 wins. They took their first division title in 16 years.

In the first round of the playoffs, Portland fell to the Memphis Grizzlies. Even worse, four of the five starters left after the season. Some were traded, while others left as free agents. The most crucial loss was Aldridge. He was Portland's all-time leading rebounder and second-leading scorer. Many experts thought Portland would be lucky to win

LEGENDS OF THE HARDWOOD

A SCORING MACHINE

DAMIAN LILLARD, POINT GUARD, 6-FOOT-3, 2012–PRESENT

In a 2014 game, Portland trailed the Sacramento Kings 117–105. With just 1:05 remaining, Damian Lillard took over. He drained three field goals, scored on a layup, and added three free throws. Lillard made those 14 points in 49 seconds. “Once I make a few, I get going,” Lillard said. But it wasn’t quite enough. The Kings held on for a 123–119 victory. “That’s the craziest game I’ve ever been a part of,” said DeMarcus Cousins of the Kings. “I don’t ever want to be in a situation with the ball in Damian Lillard’s hands. I’m glad we got the win, but that was a scary thing.”

The Trail Blazers faced the Warriors in the 2016 playoffs but could win only one game.

"[OWNER PAUL ALLEN] GOT VERY EMOTIONAL IN SAYING HE WAS PROUD OF OUR TEAM AND HOW FAR WE GOT. HE TALKED ABOUT HOW MUCH HARD WORK AND BEING TOGETHER CAN TAKE YOU."

30 games in 2015–16. In January, they seemed to be right. Portland was already 7 games under .500.

Then Stotts told his team, "I guarantee you guys, if we can be a top-15 ranked defensive team by the end of the season, we will make the playoffs." The Blazers finished with 44 wins and a playoff berth. Shooting guard C. J. McCollum averaged nearly 21 points a game. Center Mason Plumlee averaged almost eight rebounds per game. The Blazers beat the Clippers in the first round but lost in the next round to the Golden State Warriors. After the final game, owner Paul Allen choked up as he spoke to the team. "He got very emotional in saying he was proud of our team and how far we got," said shooting guard Gerald Henderson. "He talked about how much hard work and being together can take you."

But Portland couldn't maintain the late momentum. It barely made the 2016–17 playoffs and put up little resistance against Golden State. One of the few consolations was Lillard's hoisting of the Magic Johnson Award, given to the player who best combines on-court success with off-court relations with the media and general public. The team also added massive center Jusuf Nurkić in a late-season trade and looked forward to the future.

Rip City fans are among the most loyal and passionate in the NBA. Blazermaniacs feel confident that another championship banner will soon hang from the rafters of the Moda Center.

SELECTED BIBLIOGRAPHY

Ballard, Chris. *The Art of a Beautiful Game: The Thinking Fan's Tour of the NBA*. New York: Simon & Schuster, 2010.

Hareas, John. *Ultimate Basketball: More Than 100 Years of the Sport's Evolution*. New York: DK, 2004.

Hubbard, Jan, ed. *The Official NBA Basketball Encyclopedia*. 3rd edition. New York: Doubleday, 2000.

NBA.com. "Portland Trail Blazers." http://www.nba.com/blazers/.

Simmons, Bill. *The Book of Basketball: The NBA According to the Sports Guy*. New York: Ballantine, 2009.

Sports Illustrated. *Sports Illustrated Basketball's Greatest*. New York: Sports Illustrated, 2014.

WEBSITES

DUCKSTERS BASKETBALL: NBA
http://www.ducksters.com/sports/national_basketball_association.php

Learn more about NBA history, rules, positions, strategy, drills, and other topics.

JR. NBA
http://jr.nba.com/

This kids site has games, videos, game results, team and player information, statistics, and more.

Note: Every effort has been made to ensure that any websites listed above were active at the time of publication. However, because of the nature of the Internet, it is impossible to guarantee that these sites will remain active indefinitely or that their contents will not be altered.

INDEX